CONTENT

Meet Farmer Jane 4

Farmer Jane's Angry Bull 33

MEET FARMER JANE

"Our new farmer starts today," Don, the sheepdog, told the farm animals. "You must all work hard and try to behave because..."

"… she is Farmer Jane."

"This is Sam and Bertie," said Farmer Jane.

"And this is the muckiest,
muddliest farm I've ever seen!"

"What does this farm need?" Farmer Jane asked the animals.

"A spring-clean," said Farmer Jane.

Farmer Jane wrote out a long list
and pinned it to the shed door.

Number One: Muck out the shed

It's very smelly in here.
I love this muck.

Number Two: Clear up the fallen trees and branches

If I went any slower I'd be standing still.
Steady, Alice.

Number Three: Trim the sheep

Sheep are silly.

Number Four: Oil the machinery

Don's nose
won't squeak or
rust either.
The tractor
is well oiled.

Number Five: Repair the fences

It *is* getting better!

Number Six: Worm the cows

It's new stuff. All you do is pour a little...
... on to the cow's back.
That pig doesn't know anything!

Number Seven: Move the old muck heap

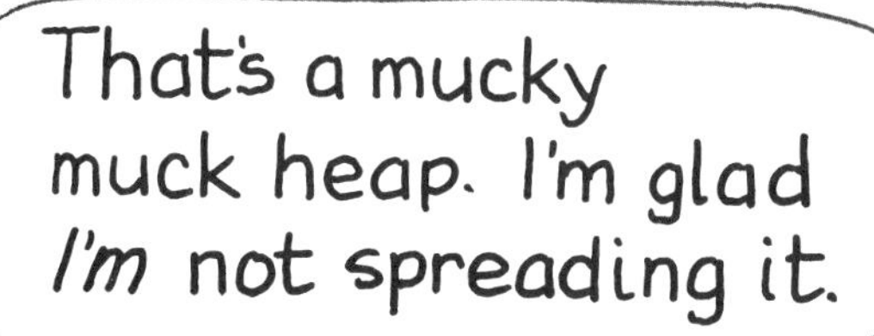
That's a mucky muck heap. I'm glad *I'm* not spreading it.

This muck heap hasn't been touched for years.
It will be perfect to spread on the fields.
to feed the crops.

Number Eight: Sow the spring crops

It's still got to flatten the soil and plant the seeds.
That tractor's puffed out.
Tractors today are spoilt. Do you remember when you ploughed the fields, Alice?

Number Nine: Brush Charlie

Charlie, you look beautiful. Alice, you're next.
I *am* beautiful.

Number Ten: Sweep the yard

Real pigs...

“What is Farmer Jane?”

“A muddy, mucky Farmer.”

“What does Farmer Jane need?”

“A spring-clean!”

FARMER JANE'S ANGRY BULL

"I'm having a rage," Charlie bellowed.

"Temper, temper," said Farmer Jane.

"I'm bored," Charlie roared. "My cold is better. I'm not staying here!"

"You are," said Farmer Jane.

"Won't and shan't" bellowed Charlie.

A-tishoo.

He charged the wall, and then charged it again. Down it crashed.

"I'm off," said Charlie.

"Bulls!" said Farmer Jane

That pig's gone quiet.

"Charlie come back," yelled Farmer Jane.

Charlie ignored her. He was having a lovely time.

"I'm a big, strong bull," he bellowed, "and I'll do what *I* want to do."

“Don, you’re a sheepdog, now you can be a ‘bull’ dog too,” puffed Farmer Jane. “Stop Charlie going into the woods and try and head him back to the yard.”

Don raced off after Charlie. When he caught up with him, Charlie laughed: “No sheepdog will ever stop me!”

And with a leap and a kick Charlie headed off towards the road.

John and the tractor had set off up the road when Charlie burst through the hedge in front of them.

"You're not going to stop me!" Charlie roared, and charged through the hedge on the other side of the road.

Charlie was beginning to feel a bit puffed. He was still wobbly from his bad cold.

"We'll go across the river, have a rest, and then go back," he thought, "when *I* decide."

Faster, Oink, faster.

Farmer Jane looked down the hill and saw Charlie standing on the middle of the bridge.

"Alice,' yelled Farmer Jane, "race down and get Charlie off the bridge. It's rotten and he's too heavy to stand on it!"

I'm a very big strong bull!

When Charlie saw Alice racing down the hill he stamped his foot in rage. He stamped so hard that his leg went straight through the bridge.

Then with a great crash and crack his other legs went through the bridge.

Some of the dust had gone up Charlie's nose and with a huge explosion – he sneezed. The bridge rocked and slithered and sank even more.

"What a messy muddle," said Farmer Jane. "Sam, run back and get the tractor and some thick ropes."

Alice looked at the bridge. “I’m strong enough to hold that up for a bit,” she said, and lent against it with all her might.

The bridge shuddered and groaned as they all waited for the tractor.

"What are we doing?" asked Sam.

"We're making a sling," said Farmer Jane, "so that Charlie can be lifted off the bridge. Who is going to swim under Charlie with the ropes?"

I'm holding up the bridge.
I'm not getting wet!
I'll go.
I can't swim.

Don jumped into the water and swam under the bridge. Bits of wood fell on top of him.

Farmer Jane took the ropes from him, climbed on the tractor bonnet, and then wriggled along the arm of the front-end loader.

Carefully she tied the ends of the ropes around it.

Everyone held their breath as Charlie was lifted into the air. Charlie held his breath *and* closed his eyes as he was gently lowered to the ground.

Can I
open my
eyes?

When they got back to the farmyard Charlie was very tired.

Farmer Jane rubbed Charlie dry. Oink spread lots of straw so he had a warm bed. Sam made him some hot food. And Don fetched a warm rug to cover him.

There's
only one
fuss-pot
here.

"A … tishoo! A … tishoo!
A … tishoo!" roared Charlie.

"Guess what?" said Farmer Jane.

"Charlie's caught another cold," said Alice.

"And can't go out," said Don.

"And will get bored!" said Sam.

"At least that bull can't fall through the bridge again," said Bertie.

Other books in this series

The Lucky Duck Song *Martin Waddell/Judy Brown*
The Little Blue Book of the *Marie Celeste* *Angie Sage*
Cyril's Cat: Charlie's Night Out *Shoo Rayner*